The Pretty Latina Girl
AND ADAM JONES

VAUGHN KOHLER

Cover and interior design—Lorie DeWorken, MindtheMargins.com

Printed in the United States of America

ISBN: 978-0-9978121-1-4

First Edition

14 13 12 11 10 / 10 9 8 7 6 5 4 3 2 1

A Very Important Word
FROM THE AUTHOR TO THE READER

In October 2007, I was hanging out at my favorite coffee shop, Bluestem Bistro, in Manhattan, Kansas, when a woman came walking through the front door. She was young and Latina and I was transfixed. What I experienced wasn't physical attraction, however; it was one of those rare moments (that I believe all men have experienced) where I was simply in awe—in a holy and innocent way—of the beauty of a member of the opposite sex. At that moment, it wasn't the spirit of Hugh Hefner that had possessed me, but the mindset of the Swiss Catholic theologian Hans Urs von Balthasar, who once wrote: "Every experience of beauty points to infinity." In other words, I saw this pretty Latina girl and my soul exclaimed, "Glory be to God!"

(Incidentally, the next time I experienced the same phenomenon was when I first saw the woman who eventually became my wife. She was praying in a Eucharistic adoration chapel, looked up, and smiled at me. Thinking about that moment, the words of C.S. Lewis come to mind: "It was like when a man, after a long sleep, still lying motionless in bed, becomes aware that he is now awake.")

At any rate, I eventually figured out the pretty Latina girl's name; but other than stupidly adding her as a friend on Facebook (she added me back!), I pursued no further contact with her.

At that time, however, I was enrolled in the creative writing program at Kansas State University. So shortly after my experience at Bluestem Bistro, I was inspired to write a short story about a rather complicated young man looking for love who one day beholds a pretty Latina girl in a coffee shop—and is absolutely captivated by her.

For the next nine years, I didn't really do anything with my short story. I did, however, notice that life went on for the real woman who inspired *The Pretty Latina Girl*. Her name is Krystal; and based on the information that showed up on her Facebook news feed, I learned that she got married and became a mama. Life seemed pretty grand for her.

But then in June 2016 I noticed that many people were posting their thoughts and prayers on her Facebook wall. I clicked on her profile to investigate and discovered that she had been diagnosed with cancer. I'm not sure why it impacted me so much to learn that. In truth, I don't really know Krystal at all. But I am a husband and a parent, and my own dad recently died of cancer. My heart went out to her and her family. I wanted to do something to help her.

After running the idea by my wife, I dashed off a Facebook message to Krystal and told her how she inspired my short story, how I wanted to publish it, and how I wanted the sales of this short story to help her family pay the high cost of her medical procedures. It took her two weeks to reply—so I figured she thought I was an idiot. But when she did, she was extremely grateful and accepted my offer. So I want you to know, my dear reader, that by purchasing this short story, you have helped a brave and beautiful young woman in her fight against cancer.

So as you can imagine, this story is very special to me and I hope you like it. Yes, the main character is a lovable weirdo, and some of the details of the unfolding plot strain credulity, but *who cares*? If the dreadful piece of writing known as *The DaVinci Code* and the utter drivel known as *50 Shades of Grey* can gain a popular and passionate following, then why not *The Pretty Latina Girl and Adam Jones*?

Best regards,

Vaughn Kohler
St. Louis, Missouri
July 2016

P.S.: If you would like to offer additional financial assistance to the real life Pretty Latina Girl and her family, please visit **vaughnkohler.com/krystal**

The Pretty Latina Girl
AND ADAM JONES

I'VE BEEN TOLD THAT I HAVE AN UNCANNY ABILITY TO MAKE THE simple complicated. My best friends Splenda and Nick once told me that I take the *Rube Goldberg* approach to human relationships. He was a cartoonist who used to draw complex devices that performed simple tasks in indirect and convoluted ways. He would design and draw a contraption full of pulleys and levers and hooks and ladders and all of these unnecessary parts would work together to ring a doorbell or flip a pancake. They say that's the perfect metaphor for the way I operate. They say I've been that way since Sydney. I don't disagree.

That's certainly what happened with the Pretty Latina Girl. She walked into my favorite coffee shop one unseasonably warm day in October. Actually, I should say she happened to it.

I had just finished swishing and swallowing the last sip of my coffee, which was lukewarm after an hour of sitting on the windowsill by my corner table. I love the view of the coffee shop from that vantage point. Built inside an old photography studio, the shop is long and rectangular, has dusty brick walls speckled with paint, large double-pane windows, and black pipes and silvery air condition ducts running along the ceiling. The floor has shoe polish flat black tile, and arranged all around the shop are a hodgepodge of tables and chairs, couches, and oriental rugs. The only things on the walls are two large beat-up cork boards, which have been pinpricked and stapled to death by advertisements for indy rock concerts and left wing political rallies. I've heard that Starbucks tries to sell not just mocha lattes, but the atmosphere and experience of sophistication. Not this coffee shop—they sell coffee, coke, and *take us or leave us*.

The shop was half full, with a richly blended crowd. There were college students with open books, church ladies with open Bibles, and businessmen with open mouths. If random soundbytes were any indication, the clientele at the coffee shop was as diverse as the furniture: "My lit professor is crazy. He wears polka dot bow ties." "I think God is trying to teach me patience and I'm not enjoying it." "Five thousand behind on my draw. I've got to rock November or I'm screwed."

At the bar, the red-headed barista named Kat, who was wearing an aqua blue t-shirt with Tweety Bird on it, put the finishing touches on a drink, slid the piping hot to-go cup to the edge of the counter and yelled, "Karen! Large Highlander Grog!" That's the last time I remember enjoying a resting heart rate.

The front door opened and as she walked in I swear there was a rush of wind and a couple of red and orange leaves cartwheeled in front of her, like giddy children running the street in a homecoming parade. She wore a cream colored sleeveless mock turtleneck, a short, grey and red plaid skirt, and had black shoes, the kind I call "witch shoes." She had long black hair with the sheen of a vinyl record. Her face was friendly and her eyes dark and lovely. The sunbeams from outside reflected in the corners of her pupils in the shape of little shining bells. Her smile was so brilliant, her teeth well ordered, like fresh linens nicely stacked in a hotel closet. But the crowning glory of this woman was her lips. My friend Jeff always used to call nice, full lips *jalapeños*, and nothing else could better describe the Pretty Latina Girl's most impressive feature. *Bonita!*

A girl like that deserved more than the conventional "Hi, I'm Adam. There's a new John Cusack movie out this Friday. Care to join me?" Somehow that seemed beneath her dignity—like giving the Blessed Virgin a chest bump.

SO WHAT ARE YOU GOING TO DO?" SPLENDA ASKED ME a couple days later in the kitchen of her little apartment, as I stretched out on the floor and she made vegetable soup.

That's not her real name, by the way. I call her that because she's always been my sugar substitute.

"I've already done it," I said.

Splenda and I aren't friends with benefits or anything. She's just a girl-space-friend who (over the years) has made the absence of a girlfriend more bearable. Actually, Splenda's a pretty cute girl herself, the kind of cute girl who inexplicably never gets asked out. She's about 5'4", a hundred and nothing, the kind of girl who's always the one cheerleading squads vault into the air during special stunts. She's got cheerful green eyes and her face is lightly dusted with freckles. When she was little, Splenda's smile was always way too big for the rest of her face. Now that she's older, it still is.

Splenda's always been at peace with who she is, but if there was anything she *really, really* liked about herself, it's her hair. And she should. She's got chestnut brown hair that falls in thick corkscrew curls that couldn't be straightened with a blowtorch. They've always been her trademark. It's usually the way she gets attention, if any, from guys. They say, "Wow, your hair is wild; kind of kinky, even." Or, "You should do, like, shampoo commercials or something."

At holidays, Splenda and I buy each other non-romantic gifts like old Michael J. Fox movies or microwave dinners. Last Christmas, we went to Mall Saint Matthews and took our picture together with the drunk Santa Claus, who served in 'Nam with the department store's owner. This guy smells like Swisher Sweets, has a stringy, yellowish beard and sucks on candy canes he's dipped in his vodka-spiked diet coke. Sometimes he gets so drunk he'll burp out the names of the reindeer for the kids. The parents don't like it.

"You asked her out?" Splenda said, a squeaky, delighted surprise in her voice. "That's great! Way to take the direct approach for once. I'm proud of you."

Splenda's always served as my own personal Tony Robbins. In eighth grade, I got cut from the soccer team and was pretty depressed about it. It's the only time I ever heard her cuss. "That Coach Santangelo," she said, red-faced and almost crying. "What a dumbass."

That may have been the most negative thing I ever heard her say—about anything or anyone. A distant second would be what she said when, after a three year relationship, Sydney dumped me at the International House of Pancakes without so much as a word of explanation: "Well, Adam, maybe it's a blessing in disguise. Maybe she doesn't deserve you."

"No," I answered. "I didn't ask her out."

"Well," she said, squinting at me in confusion. "What did you do?"

Splenda and I are kindred spirits. So I figured she'd like my idea.

"I wrote her a story."

FOUR DAYS LATER, SPLENDA, NICK AND I WERE AT THE UNION talking about the Pretty Latina girl again.

"Maddie told me you're in love," Nick said. He doesn't call her Splenda. "But I hear Rube Goldberg showed up again."

I looked at Splenda like Jesus should have looked at Judas.

"Adam," Nick said. "Why can't you just do the conventional thing and ask her out?"

Conventional is a good word to describe Nick. His full name is Nicolas Andrew Head, but he just goes by Nick Head, and isn't embarrassed to do so. None of his family seems embarrassed by their last name, even his dad, whose name is Richard. I feel sorry for them, because the joke's on them, and they don't seem to know it. I was always comforted by the fact that Nick's older sister Christy could get married and take her husband's last name. That was a legitimate way out. But one day I got her wedding invitation and when I opened it up it said she was marrying a guy named Curtis Haug. Christy is pretty independent, and a feminist, so now she's Christy Head-Haug.

"It's simple," Nick said. "Just walk up to her and do it."

Conventional and simple. That's Nick Head. Though when it comes to girls, he can afford to be, because he's got Scandinavian tennis player good looks. He's got blonde hair, clear blue eyes, and he looks like he's eaten healthy, well-balanced meals his whole life. He's also quiet, which most girls interpret as him being mysterious. But Nick Head isn't mysterious. Just quiet, conventional, and simple. Which I suppose is why we're friends. We balance each other out. Like yin and yang.

"That may work for you, Nick," I said. "But things aren't as easy for us mere mortals."

"Yeah," Splenda said, punching Nick playfully. "Not everyone attracts the opposite sex so easily."

For a long time, I've harbored the suspicion that Splenda likes Nick—a lot. A couple of years ago on Valentine's Day, when Sydney and I were still together, Splenda was home by herself and I called her to make sure she wasn't too depressed. She sighed and said she was washing her hair and feeling "ro-tic." I asked, "What's ro-tic?" And she said, "Romantic without the man." I got off the phone with her, Nick called five minutes later to ask me if I had his copy of Rocky IV, and I told him what she said. He said, "Man, I feel sorry for her. That's just not right." A week later, I found out they hung out together that night. We were watching Seinfeld when I asked them what they did. Splenda said, "Just hung out," but smiled sheepishly and looked over at Nick as if to say "tell him." But Nick said nothing and kept watching Seinfeld. "Don't give him any excuses," Nick said.

"So," he turned to me again. "You wrote her a story?"

"Well, actually, I'm writing her a story," I said. "I'm only done with the rough draft."

"What's the story about?" he asked. Splenda perked up to listen, too.

"I'll read it to you," I said.

So, I read it to them. I read to them about an eccentric but loveable twenty-five-year-old guy who saw a beautiful Latina girl in his favorite coffee shop. I read how the guy was enamored with the Latina girl so much that he thought asking her out demanded a different approach. I described how the eccentric but loveable guy wrote a story and left it anonymously on the Pretty Latina Girl's table the next time she was at the coffee shop and had excused herself to go to the restroom. Then I read to them how the eccentric guy explained in the story that if the Pretty Latina Girl was interested in the eccentric but loveable guy she could show up to the coffee shop and the eccentric but loveable guy would be reading his rare collector's copy of *The Scarlet Pimpernel*. Then they could meet. Maybe discover that they were soul mates.

Splenda actually had tears in her eyes. She's always been like that. She even bawled at *Star Trek 2: The Wrath of Khan*, when Spock died saving the ship.

"Adam," she said. "That was incredible."

"Okay," she said. "Do it. I can't imagine any decent girl not at least appreciating the gesture. I know I would."

"Well, I can't do it," I said.

'What? What!" Splenda yelled. "Why not?"

"Because," I said. "She introduced herself to me this afternoon at the coffee shop."

"Wait. What?" said Splenda. "That's terrific!"

"Yeah, man," Nick said. "You couldn't have planned that better!"

"Are you kidding me?" I asked. "Everything's messed up."

"What are you talking about?"

"What happened, Adam?" Splenda asked.

"Well," I said. "I'm at the coffee shop this afternoon and lo and behold she comes in again. I put my head down and calmly reach into my book bag for my albuterol inhaler. I'm looking down at my copy of *Date Out of Your League,* wondering if I should try looking at her more intently, to try to get more details for my story. Then, all of a sudden, I hear someone speak to me: '*I really like your shirt.*' I look up, and it's her!"

"What shirt were you wearing?" Nick asked.

"John Cusack for President," I said. "The one with the picture of him from *Say Anything.* Holding the stereo over his head."

"That's my favorite shirt of yours, too," Splenda chirped. "I love that movie."

"That what she said, too," I said.

"Congratulations, buddy," Nick said. "There's your invitation."

"Not hardly," I said. "She looked at me and said, 'Have we met before? I'm Jennifer Smits.' And I say, 'Uh, no.

People tell me I look a lot like this guy Adam Jones. They say it's uncanny.' "

Splenda and Nick's faces went blank.

"Are you nuts?" asked Nick.

"No," I said. "I told her my name was Dennis Franz."

"The actor?" Splenda said. "Where did that come from?"

"Well, she said her name was Jennifer Smits," I said. "Which, incidentally, is a very disappointing name for a Latina girl. I was really hoping for something like Maria Valero, or Teresa Cruz, or Isabel Fuentes. Maybe even the combination of a common American name with a saucy Hispanic surname—like Sarah Valdez or Linda Montes. Jennifer Smits—that was almost a deal breaker."

"I am still not following you," Splenda said. "Dennis Franz?"

"Jimmy Smits used to play one of the cops on that show NYPD Blue," I explained. "His partner was played by Dennis Franz. That's what made me think of calling myself by that name."

I looked at Splenda and Nick, searching some indication that they "got it." Nope.

"I don't understand why you called yourself anything but yourself, Adam," Splenda said. "I don't understand why you came up with that whole crazy story. You had the perfect opportunity. Now, you've gotten yourself in a lose/lose situation."

"What do you mean?"

"What are you going to do if she tries to look up Dennis Franz?" Splenda asked.

"She won't," I said. "Dennis is from out of town. He

didn't say where he was from. He's just in town for awhile visiting his sister who lives here. She's been going through months of chemo treatments, because she's dying of cancer."

"Why did you say that?" Nick asked.

"I figured the subject of death would make her want to end the conversation fast," I explained. "Things did get a little awkward. She said she was Catholic and that she'd pray a rosary for my sister, then she bought her drink and left."

"Girls don't like to be lied to, Adam," Splenda said. "I just don't think you are going to be able to sustain this stupid little story of yours. And when she figures it out, she's not going to be happy."

"I'm sorry," I said. "I just got a little nervous and let my eccentricity run wild."

"No, Adam," Splenda said. "You let your insecurity run wild."

"No, no, I didn't," I explained. "Trust me. I'm not down on myself or anything. But I just think a girl has to be prepared for me."

"What?"

"Yeah," I explained. "It's like that movie *Eternal Sunshine of the Spotless Mind*. Great movie. Powerful ending. But I know a bunch of people who won't even give it a shot because they think it's weird."

"And you think you're weird like that movie?" Splenda asked.

"*Eccentric*, yes," I said. "C'mon, Splenda—I'm a guy and I always go #1 sitting down. Sometimes I even use the handicap stall in the public restroom because it's bigger and wider and otherwise I'll get claustrophobic. I really want to find out if anything happens if I say 'bloody Mary' three times in front of a mirror, but I won't do it. Not because I'm afraid of getting killed, but I'm afraid she might show up and kill Lloyd, my yellow lab. And one time when I visited Meramec Caverns in Missouri it was all I could do not to pinch off one of those little, toothpick-sized stalactites. And you know why?"

"Why?"

"Because it takes like a billion years for those things to form. And there's a $500,000 fine and possible jail time if you vandalize them. And I couldn't help thinking how hilarious it would be if you were sitting in jail and you were surrounded by murderers and rapists and all sorts of violent criminals and they say to you, 'So, what'd they get you for?' And you get to say, 'I broke one of those toothpick-sized stalactites at Meramec Caverns.' "

"Adam," Splenda said. "Those kind of thoughts are what makes you *you*."

"Maybe so," I said. "But I just think the average girl on the street needs to know that ahead of time. That's why I included all of that information in 'The Pretty Latina Girl.' "

"What?"

"That's the name of the story I'm going to leave for her."

"Oh."

"So, what's going to happen," Nick asked. "When she finds out you're not Dennis Franz?"

"Well," I said. "I think I'm in good shape. When she introduced herself to me, I was wearing a baseball cap and contacts. And my hair is getting pretty long. So, I figure once I cut my hair and wear glasses, she won't think I'm the same guy."

Splenda blanched.

"That is never going to work, Adam!"

"Seriously, man," Nick said. "That's just stupid."

"Well," I said. "Hope—or stupidity—springs eternal."

AND HOPE—OR STUPIDITY—SPRUNG ETERNAL FOR THE NEXT six weeks. Within another day, I had revised my rough draft, polished up my final draft, and waited for the Pretty Latina Girl to show up at the coffee shop again. Within another week, she did.

The whole thing actually worked out perfectly, which I took as a sign of serendipity. I had been sitting (strategically) at a table in the far corner of the shop, the part that bends around and behind the side of the main counter. In that corner, there's a large, antique bean-roasting machine, and it halfway conceals the little table positioned right next to it.

I had to wait about forty-five minutes before she shut *Microeconomics: An Introduction to Efficiency and Productivity* and got up to go the ladies room. Feeling like a cross between a forlorn cavalier and a self-conscious stalker, I got up, hurried over to her table, did a quick but nonchalant scan to see if anyone was looking—and delivered the goods. On the way out, I flipped my cell phone open and text messaged Splenda: *did it.* She replied a minute later: *u r nuts but i luv u* ☺.

I CERTAINLY WENT NUTS WAITING FOR JENNIFER SMITS'S RESPONSE. From that day on and every day after (except Sunday), I would go and study long hours at the coffee shop, always bringing my rare collector's copy of *The Scarlet Pimpernel*. I would even pile a couple of other books on my table and lean *Pimpernel* on them, so that it looked like one of those books on display at *Barnes and Noble*. One time I even brought two copies, although the second one was just a Penguin Classics edition. I waited and waited. But the crisp chill of October turned into the genuine cold of November, and my hope and enthusiasm began to die with the coming of winter.

Then one day, as I was looking out the coffee shop window into the street, and noticing the people outside bundled up, leaning forward as they walked against the wind, their visible breaths a vain rebellion against the bitter cold, the Pretty Latina girl walked slowly and tentatively through the front door.

She spotted *The Scarlet Pimpernel*, walked over to my table, and I stood up out of politeness. She was dressed a lot nicer than a November afternoon called for—*yes!* I looked at her and smiled, but in my insecurity, shifted my eyes for a moment. When I looked back, she was still looking right at me, thoughtfully, like a woman cherishing a greeting card. I couldn't help thinking that I'd swung for the fence and hit the moon.

"I'm Adam," I said, extending my hand. "Adam Jones."

"I'm Jennifer," she said. "Jennifer Smits."

"Um," I said. "Do you want something to drink?"

"Sure," she said softly.

I ordered us two caramel apple ciders. While I was at the counter, I text messaged Splenda: *she is here im so nervous.*

Jennifer spoke with that soft, monotonous tone of voice that girls sometime use and you don't know if they are just feeling relaxed and pleasant or guarded and suspicious. I told her I was in the grad program in English. She told me she was pursuing an MBA. I shared a little bit about where I was from, my family, friends, Splenda and Nick. She mentioned that she had just gotten back from a trip to Victoria, British Columbia, and that she was part Canadian. Splenda had been wrong. The Pretty Latina Girl (who was partly Canadian) didn't suspect a thing.

"Will you please tell me what's going on?" she asked, straightening herself up in her chair, folding her hands, and resting them on the table.

"What do you mean?" I asked.

"Dennis Franz," she said. A little lump of panic began to form in my chest. "I met you a month ago and you said your name was Dennis Franz. I know it was you."

"Honestly," I said. "My name is Adam Jones. Want to see my Driver's License?"

"I know you're Adam Jones," she said. "I came in here weeks ago and asked around. No offense, but I'm a 'safety first' kind of girl and wanted to make sure you weren't some sort of pervert or stalker."

"No," I said, "I'm not either of those."

"I know," she said. "I felt better when I found that out. I asked the baristas here who the regulars were. They mentioned a guy who looks a whole lot like you and told me his name was Adam Jones. I asked, 'Could his name be Dennis Franz?' And they said, 'No, that's Adam Jones. It's got to be. He's here all the time.' I was so confused and now I'm even more confused."

She put her hands flat on the table and leaned in toward me.

"Listen," she said. "I loved your story. That's why I'm here. I was touched by it. I *am* touched by it. I mean, you are an amazing writer. I was very impressed. And the fact that you'd do that for me? Well, that's just really sweet."

"Thanks," I said.

"But when we met over a month ago, I know you told me your name was Dennis Franz. I have a very good memory. Why did you lie and tell me your name was Dennis Franz and, worse, come up with that story about your dying sister? That's not just a lie," she said. "It's creepy. Weird."

Weird. I felt like saying *eccentric*, but I couldn't speak. My heart felt like someone had just filled it with caulking. Jennifer put her elbows on the table, folded her hands as if praying, but with both index fingers pointing out. She squinted at me as I feigned ignorance, waiting for an explanation that her face said I'd never be able to come up with. Somewhere above the Patty Griffin song playing on the house stereo, I could hear Rube Goldberg chuckling his approval. His disciple, his freakshow use-a-table-saw-to-slice-a-piece-of-pizza disciple had once again murdered a perfectly good opportunity for a relationship. I had bludgeoned it to death with complication. My own actions, my own creepy, weird heart had led me to this. I felt: humiliated.

Then. Movement from the front of the shop. I noticed a young woman come through the door. She was wearing a powder blue and white winter jacket; it was long and seemed too big for her. Cream colored wool mittens kept her hands warm, and a bright red scarf wrapped several times around her neck looked like it might suffocate her. On her head she wore a thick, wool hat pulled tightly over her ears. It was also cream colored, and between the hat and the sunglasses she was wearing, you could barely see her face. Noticing my distraction, the Pretty Latina Girl turned around.

The young woman unwrapped her scarf and took off her hat and—surprised—I gasped softly. She had no hair. She tucked the wool hat into her pocket and pulled out a bright red bandana. She slid it over her forehead and tied it in a tight knot right above her neck.

The young woman ordered her drink and, waiting for her order, turned to face us. "Oh, hey!" she exclaimed. Jennifer looked at me and I shrugged my eyes.

As she walked toward us, she smiled a smile that was too big for her face. She finally took her sunglasses off and my heart fell into my stomach.

"Oh," the young woman said, "I'm so sorry. I thought you were someone else." She turned toward me. "You look so much like my brother!"

"Who is your brother?" Jennifer asked.

"Dennis Franz," the young woman said. "He's in town visiting me." The young woman looked at me and smiled. "Didn't know you had a twin out there, did you?

"Well, I'm sorry to have bothered you. Have a nice day."

"You, too."

Now it was Jennifer who looked humiliated. "Well," she said. "I guess I owe you an apology." And with that, the Pretty Latina Girl started talking about how uncanny the resemblance was between me and Dennis, how I should use this new plot twist in one of my short stories, and how she felt bad for questioning my integrity. She told me she was sorry to have called me weird, that I was obviously creative, talented, and passionate. She apologized for being so straightforward, but admitted to me that she'd really like to get to know me better. She suggested we check out the new John Cusack movie out in the theaters on Friday. She even wondered aloud if someday I'd write a novel about our relationship. "This feels like *Sleepless in Seattle*, doesn't it?" she asked. But nothing she said registered.

I was thinking about the young woman with no hair. I was thinking about how she turned back and winked at me. I was thinking about how, looking like a chemo patient shorn of her crowning glory, she walked out the front door of the coffee shop with a smile on her face.

And right before the door closed behind her, we looked at each other with a conscious acknowledgement of the years between us. The stress and sadness on my face said, "You didn't have to do this." But Splenda mouthed the words: "It'll grow back."

OUT OF POLITENESS, I EXCHANGED PHONE NUMBERS WITH Jennifer Smits, whose name seemed even more unspectacular now. I left the coffee shop and walked down the street, looking everyone in the face and catching no one's attention. I wondered if it was remotely possible that there was another guy on the planet who had written a story and given it to a girl that he wanted so badly to win, only to end up discouraged by his own success. I wondered how many lonely and forlorn souls pined after the unattainable gods and goddesses in their lives, those idols of the imagination they first encountered on their walk to work, at the gym, or in their favorite coffee shop.

I wondered if they understood how safe their fascinations were, how self-protective. I wondered if they could ever admit that chasing an impossible ideal is really the act of a coward. And I wondered if I, the Rube Goldberg of Romance, had the courage to embrace a simple truth—a truth that was now as obvious and uncomplicated as the smile on her face.

My substitute for love, I thought as I walked to find my friend, *is actually the real thing.*

About the Author

VAUGHN KOHLER is a professional writer, ghost writer, speaker, and communications consultant who considers himself "the point man for people of impact." Whether his clients are c-level executives or spiritual leaders, his mission is "to help men and women maximize their impact for their gain and the good of the world." Over the course of his life, he has been a pastor, magazine editor, marketing specialist, development director, and college-level Communications instructor. He holds degrees in communications, religion, and creative writing. He lives in St. Louis, Missouri. Find him online at **vaughnkohler.com.**

CONNECT WITH HIM:

 **Facebook** www.facebook.com/vaughn.kohler

 Twitter @vaughnkohler

 Instagram @vaughnkohler

Book Vaughn Kohler
TO SPEAK AT YOUR EVENT

VAUGHN HAS DELIVERED HUNDREDS OF MESSAGES AND presentations to nonprofit organizations, college students, church groups, and businesses.

He makes things thought-provoking, but easy-to-understand; telling stories, asking questions, using memorable analogies, and drawing from diverse sources of wisdom and insight–from Jesus of Nazareth to Steve Jobs.

He wants to equip and inspire his audiences to achieve greater success and happiness; to maximize their impact for their gain and the good of the world.

SPEAKING TOPICS

Vaughn will help you…

- Maximize your confidence to full engage those around you

- Build rapport with others to build a better career, business, and life

- Infuse every interpersonal encounter with magic and meaning

- Transform the world through compelling acts of kindness

SPEECHES, SEMINARS, ETC.

To get on Vaughn's schedule,
send an email to **vaughn@vaughnkohler.com**

www.vaughnkohler.com